François le Foutre

THERE'S SEAMEN ON THE POOP-DECK!

BOOK 1 OF
The Seamen Sexology

THE SEAMEN SEXOLOGY

Book 1: There's Seamen on the Poop-Deck!
Book 2: My Coxswain Is Bigger Than Yours
Book 3: Too Many Fingers in the Dyke
Book 4: The Best Sextant I Ever Had (March 2018)

For books, exclusive content, merchandise, dates, and more, enlist at www.seamensexology.com.

Standing on My Poop

IT WAS A HOT DAY, and I spent it as I spend most hot days—standing on top of my poop.

I allow no one to stand on my poop-deck, except by special invitation, and by then my men knew it. The last time a man had tried to come on my poop without permission, the other men took it upon themselves to come all over him and beat him off. He lay humiliated for over an hour underneath all my seamen—they even talked of drowning him—but he took his punishment well, and after that none even dared ask to stand on my poop. Why, even the mere suggestion would produce a wrinkled brow and an upturned nose, as if the very thought offended them.

So there I stood, on top of my poop, looking down on my men. They worked on their knees, gazing up at me from time to time with eyes of admiration, as they sang one of their favorite sea shanties—"The Stiffer the Sailor the Harder the *Foc.*"

I wanted to be a wise man, you see
So I went to the university
Yes I went to the fac to take a crack
At a life with an education track
I studied so well, I could have gone if
I hadn't been nervous and gotten so stiff
They thought I was crazy, they called me a hack,
The stiffer the sailor the harder the fac

La fac, la fac, I went to a fac
But the stiffer the sailor the harder the fac.

1

I wandered the trees, came upon the seas
Since I'd been turned out from universities
I saw fish and whales—but only the tails
In the year I spent underneath all those sails
But the one I like best, la phoque—leave the rest
O! pinniped mammals with you I'm obsessed
But look at them hard and they'll run off in shock,
The stiffer the sailor the harder the phoque

La phoque, la phoque, I just want a phoque
But the stiffer the sailor the harder the phoque.

Now I'm a sailor, a seaman you see,
'Cause I never went to university
From the tip of the boom to the mast so upright
I spend all day pulling the foc oh so tight
Straighten your arms, pull with your might
Pull it and pull it and pull it so tight.
Straighten your arms till your elbows lock,
The stiffer the sailor the harder the foc

Le foc, le foc, I want a tight foc
The stiffer the sailor the harder the foc.
Le foc, le foc, I want a tight foc
The stiffer the sailor the harder the foc.

As my men reached their climax, I gave a grin, pleased as I was with the work they had done. Fully satisfied, I stepped off my poop, wiped my boots on my poop mat, and descended into the belly of the *Raging Queen*.

ROLLING IN MY POOP

*T*HE *RAGING QUEEN* had two openings—one in the front, at the mouth of the ship, and a smaller opening at the rear. The rear entrance had always been my favorite. The passage was long and narrow, with a smooth finish. I am not the largest of men, but even so it was always a tight fit, which made it quite the experience. It was as if as I entered her, she was squeezing me tight, willing me never to go.

I ran my hands along her through the length of her corridor, fingering her delicately in a loving embrace. My *Raging Queen* moved up and down underneath me in undulating waves, almost shuddering under my touch. She creaked and moaned, screamed and gyrated, and though she was for now under the control of my seamen, it was I, only I, whose every order she followed. She submitted to me first, always to me, and I liked it that way.

Yes, it was safe to say that every time I entered the *Raging Queen*, I fell in love with her all over again.

I took a few steps and then paused a moment. Never wanted to go in too far at once. Better to do it slowly, a little bit at a time. Build up the anticipation, tease her almost. She moaned louder. Bucked harder. Screamed with more fury. I had her right where I wanted her.

I began to hear the mutterings of the men above me. That might have distracted a lesser man, but to me it only made me want to go slower. I never shied away from being caught with my *Raging Queen*.

Finally, with deeper penetration on every step, I reached the poop cabin.

Most men are proud of their poops. How large they are, how beautiful they are upon close examination. Why, every rear admiral

I met within minutes would ask me if I wanted to see his poop. Of course I would accept—you never decline a man's invitation to show you his poop—and whether it was a clean poop or a messy poop, we'd spend the next several hours examining every inch of it, even playing games in it from time to time. Poker was a popular one. I've lost count of the number of times I've pokered in a man's poop.

But while every man is proud of his poop, I happened to think mine was especially delightful. It was larger than most, and I boasted that over one hundred different kinds of woods had been inside it—dark woods and light woods, hard woods and soft woods, rough woods and smooth woods, strong woods and loose woods. There were traces of each all throughout my poop, most of which had been acquired during my various world travels: an Akan fertility doll, dark brown with a large round head, given to me by a long, thin Indian; a trunk of African ebony; dozens of light, softwood rodents which still tickled my fancy; and a massive horsehair rope that hung from the ceiling and seemed to impress all with its girth. I'd grown to love the darker, harder, rougher woods the best, so those were the ones I brought into my poop the most, but really I'd put anything strong or unique in there if it would fit.

My poop, of course, was where I took my meals, so all my food would end up there eventually. I brought in all different kinds of nuts, and meats, and the odd vegetable when I was in the right mood. And all of these would combine to give my poop a wonderful oaky aroma, which filled my nostrils with a musky bouquet.

Yes, I loved my poop, and I spent as much time in there as possible.

The shelf just inside my poop contained books, so coming in this evening I selected one at random and took it to my seat—a narrow object of porcelain, which the Chinese say is a seat for the gods. I sat proudly and opened the tome, resting it on my widened knees to carry its massive weight. Presently, there was a knock at the door.

He was early.

I smiled and immediately stood. Fortunately I had not yet started reading—it's very awkward being interrupted while reading in my poop cabin, though depending on the mood of myself and my partner, sometimes it works out just the same. Regardless, I had not yet started on this occasion, so his timing was perfect.

I opened the door, standing tall and puffing out my chest to make myself look bigger. "Mmmm," I whispered. "Please come in." I stepped aside to allow him to enter, but the boy stood there sheepishly, almost embarrassed. This happened from time to time.

The boy in question was our newest shipmate. He was a slight young man of eighteen, not quite fully formed in the chest and shoulders. His skin was red, sunburned from a day out at sea after a lifetime indoors. He wore fine clothing that had not yet been broken in.

"Don't be shy," I said. "For the rest of today, my poop is your poop."

"*Oui, monsieur.*"

"Please. Call me 'le Foutre.'"

He came in.

"Sit. Here, use my porcelain chair—"

"No, I couldn't—"

"I insist." I presented him with the seat. He slowly sat in it, and widened his knees, as one does when sitting on porcelain. "Nice, isn't it?"

He nodded. "*Oui, monsieur* . . . Foutre."

Now for the tricky part. He had made it as far as my room, but I had to make him feel comfortable if I was to put my designs on him. First step, small talk.

"You come from a wealthy family?" I asked. He shifted in his seat, unsure how to answer. I could play this game. "Lords?" He shook his head. "Clerks?"

"Clergy."

"Ooh, my favorite. And you ran away from the church." He nodded. "Because father and mother—or should I say father and sister—would not admit that you existed."

He was quiet a moment, wanting to give me everything but not sure if he should. Finally, he opened up. "He was an archbishop."

"Oh my."

The commotion upstairs was getting louder, but I paid it no attention. I moved closer to him and put my hand on his. "Do not fear. The *Raging Queen* rejects no one. And we judge no one, either."

"I've never been with anyone before, sir."

I had suspected as much. "At least you're starting off with your yacht in the right harbor," I said. I took his face in my hand. Turned it toward me. He moved in. Kissed my lips. He was soft at first, then kissed me harder.

This was going to be easier than I'd thought.

Then, it was as if a demon took him over. He pawed at me as if possessed, nearly two decades of pent-up regression, a score of denied existence, eighteen years being refused any satisfaction to a thousand human urges, fighting to make their way out all at once. He pushed me backward, and we crashed onto the floor. He landed on top of me and pinned me down, the surges of the moment giving him an unprecedented strength, and one he likely wouldn't be able to repeat until months of pole-pulling and rope-tugging had passed. This was a special moment for him, and he was controlling it through his uncontrollable liberation.

His tongue entered my mouth, not so much exploring it as burrowing into it. I fought back, and he moved to my neck, biting like a vampire. I dug my fingernails into his shoulder blades, to which he responded by sucking on my flesh even harder. The noise of the sea and of the seamen upstairs was by now a full roar; he could surely feel the strength of my member—I certainly felt his—and he reached his hand down to grasp it through my hosen. He squeezed, then reached through my braes to take the whole thing into his bare hand. He held it there for a moment, gasped and looked into my eyes—part excitement, part intimidation—and then freed it from its cloth prison. He shifted his gaze down to my lance, and the look turned to one of pure lust before he dropped his head all the way down to my pubic bone, sending my meat to the back of his throat.

It was a huge, huge shock. How could a boy who had looked so innocent not five minutes ago be capable of such an advanced display of skill? But the thought quickly left my mind as he tongued my cherries, as if licking the salt off a massive pair of chestnuts with a banana still in his throat. His lips clamped around me. I grabbed the back of his head, gripped his hair between my fingers, wrapped my legs around his neck, and then . . . and then—

A cry from upstairs: *"There's seamen on the poop-deck!"*

What? I must have misheard. There's never any seamen on my poop unless specifically invited. I put the thought quickly out of my mind, though, as the boy reached his hand through the openings in my hosen and my braes, placing a finger against my cul-de-sac. I willed him to put it farther.

"Yes," I cried. "Do it. *Do it!*"

"There's seamen on the poop-deck!"

"But I haven't come up there!" I cried, loud enough to be heard over the commotion.

"No, pirates!"

The boy's finger went all the way inside me, up to the third knuckle. My beef was still completely down his throat, and I wrestled with my will as he played me from both sides like a hornpipe.

But I could not get the thought out of my head: that there was unwanted seamen on my poop. "Stop," I said.

He didn't.

"Stop!" I insisted. I grabbed him by the hair and tried to pull him away from me, but he grabbed my backside with his free hand and held me tight, resisting with superhuman strength and imbedding a second finger all the way into my hole.

I gave in and allowed him to continue his digital Greeking. After a few more minutes of commotion, all was quiet upstairs, the boy and I had collapsed in a sweaty, crumpling heap, and I was crying in a way that I had not done since the day I lost my virginity to that Finnish scullery maid twenty years before.

BUT, PIRATE!

HE BOY AND I lay for some time in each other's arms, both glowing amorously. Most men of his age have some feelings of remorse, or at least confusion, after a first experience such as this. All would have asked for some kind of reciprocation. But I had given him none, and yet he continued to smile, a boy of profound generosity, one that could only be the product of clergy, I supposed.

In time, the memory of the commotion upstairs came back into my mind. There had been something about seamen on my poop-deck, and all my men knew you never came on my poop without permission. There was something else I'd heard, too—about privates, I think it was—and as quiet as it was now, I was beginning to feel nervous.

"I need you to move," I said, softly as possible, shifting uncomfortably underneath the boy. "I have an itch I need to scratch." He put his hand back on my danglies and scratched the hair. That felt better, and now that it was taken care of, it was time to investigate what had been going on upstairs during our blanket drill. I moved again, and he rolled over, letting me stand. I helped him up, overcoming the weakness in my knees, and then tucked myself in.

I held out my hand. "Shall we?"

He took it, and we left my poop, going out the same way we came, through the smooth, narrow passageway all the way at the rear of the ship. I opened the exit—amazed, as always, at how much easier it is to exit the rear than it is to enter—and was just getting ready to turn to my mate and comment on that when I was seized by both arms.

Quoi le foutre?!

Then I saw him. My arch-nemesis and part-time lover.

"Captain Standish," I hissed.

"That's Aaaaaaadmiral Standish now, Foutre."

For fifteen years, Cocksmith Standish had been the laughing stock among pirates. His pants were too tight, his shirts were too frilly, his hat was too fashionable, and his doublet too colorful. He always prided himself on his appearance, and that made him the butt of most pirates' jokes.

It seemed that, finally, he'd had enough and was demanding some respect. "Oh, you've bypassed Commodore and gone straight to Rear Admiral?" I said.

"I'm not a rear admiral. I'm a vice admiral!" he roared.

"Rear admiral would have been more fitting," I replied. "You always were a butt-pirate."

He threw a fist into my stomach, knocking the wind out of me.

"Y' might want to be quiet if y' don't want more o' that," he said. "I trust you enjoyed your time with my rear gunner here." The boy stepped to his side, a smile of satisfaction on his face. I was devastated. Here I'd thought we had a real connection, but it was all just a ruse. He'd been playing with me, just so he could take my *Raging Queen* away. "As you can see, while you were down there, we raised the pole and tightened the jib—what do you call it? The *foc*. Yes, it's a much harder *foc* than your men are capable of."

"Congrats on getting the pole up to full mast. The times you and I have been together it's never gotten higher than half."

He hit me again, but this time I saw it coming and tensed my stomach to take the blow.

"He doesn't know!" he said to his men. "We've never done that!"

"I know you fancy yourself a man of the navy, but you've never been very proud below the navel."

He seethed. Good. I liked him that way. It would make things better . . . later. I knew there would be a later. There always was.

He turned to his navigator. "Change our heading," he said. "Set sail for Lapland."

"No!" I cried. "Not Lapland! Anywhere but Lapland!"

And he smirked with the satisfaction of finally having gotten under my skin. "Take him to the fo'c'sle," he said to the men who held me. "It's already full of his seamen, might as well give it a little more."

And they carried me off, screaming toward the fore of my *Raging Queen*.

A Fo'c'sle Full of Seamen

STANDISH'S GOONS DRAGGED ME down the main deck, past the cockboat and toward the fo'c'sle. Unlike many captains, I'm no stranger to my fo'c'sle, having entered it many times in the past. But being forced toward it is a whole different experience.

There was a barrier blocking the entrance, watched over by two more of Standish's men—big hairy bears, with massive chests and buttocks. One of them removed the barrier, and then the other dug his fingers into the fo'c'sle opening and pulled it wide. It made me grimace to see him being so rough with my *Raging Queen*, but he was a brute and a boar, clearly with very little experience opening fo'c'sles, and there was nothing I could do about it now. I would have my way with him eventually. Oh, yes, I would finish up on top.

I was thrown inside the fo'c'sle and into a crowd of men, the hatch slamming behind me like the breaking of a giant wind, and the barrier being dogged down. It took a moment for my eyes to adjust to the darkness, but when they did I could see, plain as the color on a virgin's backside, that I was now trapped in a fo'c'sle full of my seamen.

There's nothing wrong with being one seaman among many—after all, one seaman is often all it takes to change the whole course of a man's life. But to be trapped in there involuntarily was cause for concern. Here we all were, with no plan of escape—and worse, with the knowledge that my dutiful, loyal *Raging Queen* was on her way to Lapland under the control of one with no respect for her limits—and we had no choice but to submit one hundred percent to his bidding.

We had questions for one another—my seamen and I. It was not our first time to have so many seamen in the fo'c'sle at once, and if we were to escape our chains it would be important for us to share with one another how we'd gotten into this mess. I told them all about how the boy had come into my poop and seduced me. How it was an amazing, life-altering experience. I shared every detail about the way he held me at the back of his throat, licking my boo-boos with his tongue, shooting both fingers into my barrel, and tickling me as he did so. They listened with rapt attention, salivating over every detail, asking me question after question about how he was able to do all of that and whether he even had a gag reflex. I said that I did not know, I'd never experienced such behavior before, even with all my travels, but that surely if it was possible for one, it was possible for many, and they should practice until they were able to do it, too.

We were all weak in the knees by the time I was done sharing my side of the tale, and truth be told our mouths were a little dry and crusty in the corners. But we needed to move on.

My first mate took on the task of informing me what had happened on top.

"*Amiral*, not moments after you left for your afternoon poop, we spotted a dinghy in the distance, not far from our heading. As it got larger, we noticed that the dinghy seemed to be having trouble. It was drooping over most flaccidly, as if it could not get itself fully upright. Naturally, we were concerned about the health and stamina of the dinghy."

"Naturally," I agreed.

"So we went toward it. It got bigger and bigger the closer we got, but still, it would not come fully erect. And so we determined to give it the help it deserved. We put all hands on deck to help bring the dinghy erect. And those who were not involved were watching with fascination."

"Naturally," I said.

"Naturally. And as much attention as we were paying to the dinghy in front of us, we failed to notice the massive hermaphrodite brig coming upon our stern."

"Agh. I hate hermaphrodite brigs."

"I know. They are so confusing."

"What kind of rig do you want? Square or triangular? Why can't you just pick one?"

"Seriously. Anyway, the hermaphrodite came upon our rears so fast we barely saw it, and by the time we did, it was too late. The pirates were all over us. In only seconds, there were countless seamen on your poop-deck. And there was nothing we could do. We certainly couldn't fight—I mean, we're only navy."

There was a general grumbling of agreement from the other men.

"We tried to run around them to confuse them, and maybe make them dizzy, but they rounded us all up and put us in here."

It was quiet for a long time after he finished his tale. The men were saddened by their position, and they were sad for their *Raging Queen*. That she would be manhandled so indelicately—and worse, that she would have to go to Lapland of all places; Lapland, for God's sake!—left us all frustrated and confused, and sorry for her misfortune as well as ours.

After a long quiet, the silence was broken by a low voice at the back of the fo'c'sle.

A fo'c'sle full of seamen,
A fo'c'sle's where I want to be.
To be one of many, a million and twenty
Seamen in a bucket on the sea.

Though we all knew the song well, as slow as he was singing it, and as low as he was singing it, it had a much more melancholy air to it than normal. But another voice began to join in.

A fo'c'sle full of seamen,
There's no place that I'd rather be
Than surrounded by seamen, both slavemen and freemen,
There's nowhere my mind is so free.

And then more joined in.

I could have anchored when we were in Rome
Shown you my backside and headed on home.
I could be looking at dirt or at loam
But I love to be in the thick of the foam.
I love to be in the thick of the foam!

And now we were all chanting the song in the upbeat manner, pumping along to the music like the men I know so well.

A fo'c'sle full of seamen,
This is where I'd rather be.
There's no job that's greater, circumnavigator
It's the only lifestyle for me.

A fo'c'sle full of seamen,
The one place that fills me with glee.
To be one of many, a million and twenty
Seamen in a bucket with thee.

We sang songs for hours. We sang until the sun no longer shone inside our fo'c'sle. We sang until we no longer heard the pirates carousing. We sang until our spirits were lifted and our voices were gone—and until the lock came off and the hatch opened and Admiral Standish stood there, his big brown eyes staring into the space.

COMING OUT OF THE CLOSET

*A*s he stood on the threshold, grabbing hold of the knob to steady his balance, it was clear that Standish was on the backside of sobriety.

"Come out've y'r closet, Foutre," he slurred.

"I've been out for years," I said. "Perhaps it's your turn—"

"That's not what I meant!" His inebriated eruption almost sent him backward, but he gripped the knob harder. "I want to go into . . . as you would say . . . your poop."

"My poop."

"Aye."

"You want to go into my poop?"

"Aye, your poop. Your poop cabin. At the back of the ship. The stern."

"Oh! *La poupe!*"

"Stop toying with me, Foutre!"

"Of course. I love my poupe. As have you every time you've seen it."

"Aye."

I left the fo'c'sle, breaking free of its musky odor and smelling once again the fresh air. It was cold—clearly our latitude had risen. I've always hated the north. I prefer the nether regions of the globe, half of them anyway.

The two bears were still on either side of the fo'c'sle opening, watching us with rapt attention. I turned back to my men, nodding in solidarity as I did. They nodded back at me. Then I turned to Standish. "Nice grip you have on that knob there," I said. "You may wish to grip it harder."

He looked down at his hand and then let go, looking up. He

pointed his tactile member at me and then behind me, addressing one of the guards. "He's takin' me to show me 'is wood, y' understand."

"Aye, Admiral."

"Don't you go spreadin' no false lies."

"Nay, Admiral."

He grabbed my hand and led me back to the poop, where I would, indeed, show him every inch of wood I possessed.

He gripped my digits hard as we went along the main deck. I began to shiver, partly from the cold and partly from anticipation. To the starboard side of the ship, far off in the distance, I could make out a flicker of light—perhaps a lighthouse off the western coast of Norway. No doubt we had picked up the Norwegian sea current coming up from the south, as the wind at our backs was as hard as Standish himself. As with everything Standish did, our journey to Lapland was being made with great haste.

In a moment we were inside and following the long, narrow corridor to my poop. He clawed the walls as he walked. I grimaced—almost said something—but sometimes we must simply grin and bear it through the pain.

We reached the door, and he looked at me in drunken arousal. "Well? Open up." Though his words were slurred, his voice was gruff and guttural, as always.

I gently reached my hand out and eased open the door.

"Dammit, hurry up already!" He forced the entry, jamming me painfully inside and then himself after.

He threw the door closed behind us and grabbed me by the collar. "On your knees, boy"—and with that he kicked my feet out from under me so I fell to my knees before him. He reached his hand to fumble with his hosen, but I touched his fingers gingerly.

"No, no," I said. "Allow me."

I slipped through and pulled out his belly ruffian. It was still flaccid, but we would correct that momentarily. And Standish, for all his faults, has never been lacking in confidence, inspired or otherwise.

At the tender age of four, I'd gotten into a fight with a large Viking. He picked me up and threw me much farther than it is appropriate to throw a four-year-old, and I landed with my face perfectly sideways on a spike. Had I fallen slightly otherwise, the spike might have gone through my neck and killed me. A fraction of an inch in any direction and it would have shattered my jaw beyond repair. It could have taken out my tongue, leaving me incapable of performing my favorite activity of them all. But instead it hit the corner of my jaw, tearing the ligaments that connected the jaw on one side and going straight through my mouth to the ligaments at the opposite corner, too. As a result, I've been able ever since to open my mouth much wider than normal—a talent that has come in handy on hundreds of occasions just like this one.

I took all of him past my lips—bangers, mash, and all—and held him inside, juggling the three bits and pieces of him with my tongue like an oral circus performer. His inspiration lifted, and he began to perform my favorite trick—growing to full morning glory without ever leaving the confines of my oral sanctum. A third, a half, three-quarters, seven-eighths. He threw his head back and groaned—that loud war cry coming from the pit of his stomach—and finally his weeping willow became a full sequoia in the estuary that was my mouth.

I released him, grabbed his culty gun in my hand, and started playing it like a fiddle bow. His knees buckled underneath him; he was no longer able to maintain his strength, so moved was he by the tune I was playing on his proud pocket pipe.

I heard the patter of footsteps outside. It was ever so soft, and Standish was so hard that there was no way he could have heard it. But I was quite aware of the revolution that was already under way as Standish stood proud under me.

Moving between his legs, I inhaled Standish's oyster once more, playing with his pearls and willing him to open up his shell.

The patter became louder. I sucked him harder. Prepared his gun to fire. And fire it did.

He let out a roar so powerful it could have come from a thousand tongues and not just one. His cry shook the tables, it shook the chairs, it made the whole *Raging Queen* shudder in climactic embrace, and as it did so, Standish's cannon exploded inside my mouth, firing a million rounds into my throat. I swallowed, and as I did, yet another loaded-up wad fired. And then a cry from upstairs—

"*There's seamen on the poop-deck!*"

"No!" cried Standish. "It's in the poop cabin!"

"Sailors!" came the reply. "Up here!"

"What?!" Standish jumped to his feet, dribbling love juice down his costume in his rush to stand. "Foutre, what have you done?"

"I simply returned the favor your rear gunner did for me."

Standish's eyes widened in hate. He threw open the door and stumbled down the corridor to the main deck.

There's Seamen on the Poop-Deck!

HE SIGHT THAT MET STANDISH when he escaped the poop was one of pure pandemonium. The mizzenmast was now halfway lowered, and the pirates' flag had fallen all the way to the main deck. Standish's pirates were running around half-naked, horrified and disgusted, as my seamen, naked but for the patriotic war paint disguising their genitals, chased them unceasingly. Some of my seamen covered the pirates completely. They ruthlessly cannibalized them beyond the point of shame. The pirates screamed, they cried, they closed their eyes and covered their faces as if that would stop the gruesome activity being performed upon them. But it would not. No, their fate had already befallen them, and they were destined to live the rest of their lives unable to release the memory of that penetrating violation.

When I saw the look of shame and humiliation on Standish's face as he looked upon the scene, I smiled with satisfaction. He ran into the thick of my seamen and screamed out, "Hold, men! Hold!"

"We're trying," one of my sailors said.

And then Standish saw the boy. He was between Standish and myself, like the meat in a sandwich, eying me with admiration.

"Capture him!" Standish barked, gesturing to me. "Handcuff him to the jib."

Unlike my bedroom antics, my reply came quickly: "I don't think handcuffing me to the *foc* would give you quite the result you hope for, Cocksmith."

The boy stood there unmoving. He smiled at me. The happy meat in a human sandwich. I've always loved being part of a sandwich, even the bread. Standish looked between us. One of my sailors in the background sat on a pirate's face, muffling his screams.

The boy shuffled up to me. I lifted his chin. "You've done well," I said.

"Wha—?" Standish said. "How?"

"Your plan was effective, Standish, but you failed to consider: You did not really think that an experience such as the one he and I shared would leave him choosing you over me, did you? The moment a man enters my poop, he's mine forever. He was simply waiting for the opportune moment to distract your bearish guards, open the fo'c'sle, and launch our full-scale midnight mutiny."

Standish's jaw dropped open. It was so sexy. And the orgiastic brawl reaching its epic climax behind him didn't hurt. He looked around for an escape, but sometimes, in a situation such as this, it's too late to do anything but run.

"To the cockboat!" he cried.

"No!" I screamed. "No one touches my cock without permission."

"To the cockboat, men! It's our only salvation!"

"No means no, Cocksmith!"

I seized him by one arm. The boy took him by the other, that superhuman strength coming in handy once more, and together we threw Standish over the edge, sending him plunging into the depths of the sea. The other seamen followed suit, taking the plunge, escaping of their own accord. One by one, and a thousand at once, they shot out of my *Raging Queen*.

I looked down proudly at my handiwork, watched for a moment the swirling patterns made by seamen in the water, and then turned to my first mate.

"Mate!" I cried. The men began yet another round of fishing for the brown trout. "And then, once you're done, set course for the Netherlands!"

I held out my hand. The boy took it in his. And we entered my *Raging Queen* together.

The End

EXCERPT FROM

My Coxswain is Bigger Than Yours

BOOK 2 OF
The Seamen Sexology

There's a Dinghy in Our Rear!

*S*INCE MY MOST recent conquest over now-Admiral Cocksmith Standish, the man who seemed to come on and in my poop every time I wasn't looking, I had been a very busy boy. I had dominated three other enemies, my men bringing them to their knees and making their ships go down on them; I rescued a confused young frigate captain who wrecked on the shores of Cornwall's Shag Rock; I supported a raid on the German town of Weener, leading a transport flotilla of very hetero army men there and back and devirginizing half of three platoons; and now, I was back on my *Raging Queen*, taking it home to Stiff, Bretagne, following a weeklong panty raid on the Scilly Isles.

Under normal conditions, the trip could have been made in less than a day, but the wind died almost completely the moment Peninnis Head was out of sight, and we'd been drifting ever since. After several hours of hitching and hoisting and heaving our futtocks, making every attempt to catch any break of wind, the heat got to us. Leading Seaman Ladouche was the first to strip off his shirt, and the pleasure that brought to both him and his several voyeurs led to the latter stripping off theirs. Before we knew it, we were exposing each other's hindquarters and taking turns flogging one another with a boys' pussy.

A boys' pussy, for those unfamiliar with traditional means of naval castigation, is a smaller version of the cat-o'-nine-tails. It was typically used to punish boys, as distinct from men, but since we had no young boys on the *Raging Queen* (we do have some bounds of propriety after all), ours tended to be used more for recreational purposes such as this one. The cat-o'-nine was strictly for corporal punishment. Or, for one who had attained not so high a rank, private punishment. Or, for one being flogged out of the public eye, also private punishment. Or, for one being flogged in his nether regions, privates punishment. Or, for contracted sailors commissioned by the government who just wanted a little fun time, privateer punishment.

Alright, we might just as easily have used the cat-o'-nine in a circumstance like this, but at the moment we hadn't yet pulled it out, and we were flogging each other with a boys' pussy, rolling dice to determine which body part would bear the punishment, and for how many lashes. One of our spanks (what we call our newest seamen, when they first come out of cadet school) had just rolled double-sixes and presented us his long john as the appropriate response, when someone called—

"There's a dinghy in our rear!"

"Well, clean it out first," a voice called back.

"No, a dinghy! Back here. In our stern!"

It was our coxswain, Dorian Trim, who had spotted the dinghy and made the cry—not a surprise under the circumstances. Anytime the rest of us started playing these types of games, we could often find the slender young coxswain, never one to stray from work, sequestered somewhere far away from the action. Usually down below, Trim was discovered on this occasion positioned under the spanker, ready for whatever might blow our way.

Some men get embarrassed when stray dinghies appear on their aft sides. Personally, I've always felt that it's just a reality of the trade, one that must be borne with as much dignity and grace as possible. The bigger an officer gets, the higher and taller in rank, the more he recognizes that truth, and I was on top of a good many men, so I recognized it well. Nevertheless, it's a condition that must be addressed, so now that I knew our stern had a dinghy on it, action had to be taken. I left the games, mounted my poop-deck, and followed the good eye of my coxswain.

Sure enough, there it was. Unmistakable. A small, abandoned, brown vessel, shaped like a berry—or perhaps an egg—floating right behind us.

"Did we pass it without even noticing?" I asked.

"Maybe it passed us," Trim said.

"Whoa." The *Raging Queen* passing a dinghy was quite common, but a dinghy passing the *Raging Queen*? That seemed scientifically impossible.

But the Coxswain continued: "I'm really not sure. I'd just come out here to bight the spanker when I saw it."

Now, I do have rules of engagement for how I treat the foreign objects that come upon my *Raging Queen*. It doesn't matter the size or importance—whether it's a full, firm longboat or some random piece of flotsam—an investigation should always be conducted. More than once have I been able to identify the original owner, find him, seduce him, and then return him to his property. But in case I needed any more reason to mount the dinghy, Coxswain Trim spoke again: "There's blood on there, Admiral."

So there was. A bloody dinghy to our rear. A grim sight, indeed.

MERCI!

Lillian, my muse.

Oskar, Carlos, Amberberry, Craven, Igor, and Seamus for letting me beat you off all these years.

The fans of the Combat Tournament of Sherwood, for making sure François always comes out on top.

Steven, Estephania, Richard, JudzDesign, and Nathan for making François look (three snaps in the shape of a Z) fabulous.

And of course, *tout le monde* who made this book so successful, I had to make it a sexology. You get all the kisses.

Anti-gay bullying is real.
If you or someone you know
is being bullied, call
The Trevor Project at (866) 488-7386
or visit www.TheTrevorProject.org.

THE SEAMEN STORE

Coxwain T-shirt
Coxwain Baby T

Salty T-shirt
Salty Tanktop

Seamen T-shirt

Dyke T-shirt

Fleur-de-peen
Travel Tumbler

I Taste François Mug

For merchandise and other goodies, visit
www.seamensexology.com.